JOEL: GROWING

Dodd, Mead & Company · New York

UP A FARM MAN

Text by Patricia Demuth · Photographs by Jack Demuth

Our thanks to each and every one of the Hollands for warmly admitting us to their lives, and especially to Joel for his good-natured cooperation while we shadowed him for a year; to Burl and Marge Lethlean for providing our family a cozy country home and good neighbors; to Ellen Keller for her encouragement during the hard times; and to our sons, Daniel and Luke, for their adventurous adaptation to the farm.

1 2 3 4 5 6 7 8 9 10

Library of Congress Cataloging in Publication Data

Demuth, Patricia.
    Joel, growing up a farm man.

    Summary: Focuses on a thirteen-year-old boy who works on his family's farm, caring for livestock, harvesting hay, and preparing to manage the farm himself one day.
    1. Farmers — Illinois — Scales Mound — Juvenile literature. 2. Farm life — Illinois — Scales Mound — Juvenile literature. [1. Farmers.   2. Farm life — Illinois. 3. Occupations]   I. Demuth, Jack, ill.   II. Title.
HD8039.F32U63   630'.9773'343   81-43218
ISBN 0-396-07997-0   AACR2

Dedicated to our mothers, Anastasia Brennan and Belle Demuth

ON JOEL'S FARM

It was 11:15 at night when Joel, reading in bed, heard his mother call up, "Joel, come and feed Lamby, will you?" She usually fed the orphaned lamb, but tonight she had come home late from a meeting and did not want to go to the barn wearing good clothes.

The family dog, Jessica, jumped up from the doorstep as Joel came outside, a pair of overalls pulled over his pajamas, the laces of his boots dangling loose. "Hey, Jess," he greeted her, ruffling the dog's thick fur with one hand as they loped together to the barn. In his other hand he carried Lamby's meal—milk replacement in a soda-pop bottle capped by a black nipple.

The March air was cold and the yard light caught the mist of Joel and Jessica's breaths. A dim crescent moon hung low over the east hayfield. Otherwise, the night was black.

"Here, Lamby," called Joel, opening the door to the barn where the sheep are kept in the winter. The lamb sprang up from her warm straw bedding and sucked down the bottle in thirty seconds. Her mother had died giving birth to her a week before.

This may have been Joel's thirty-three-thousandth trip to a barn, since he goes in and out of barns at least ten times a day. Joel knows these farm buildings better than he knows his own bedroom. He surely spends more waking hours in them. He knows how to care for the animals they shelter as well as he knows how to care for himself. Farming is Joel's world.

Joel Holland has lived on this 245-acre farm since he was born, thirteen years ago. It is the farm of his ancestors. He lives in the house that his great-grandfather built. The land he helps his father and brothers farm is land that his great-great grandfather James Holland bought in 1860. James was an Irish immigrant. He drove a team of

*Jessica, a mixed-breed dog, waits eagerly as Joel prepares
for chores after school.*

*Joel drives a hog carrier down the Holland lane, one-third mile long.
Their home and ten farm buildings are all east of the lane.*

horses to plow the land and make it ready for corn. Now, five genera-
tions later, Joel plows the same land atop a John Deere tractor that
has the power of 120 horses. The rich, black soil has been pampered by
Hollands for over 120 years. Farming it is Joel's heritage.

The Holland farm is near Scales Mound, a tiny town of 400 people
snuggled in the northwestern corner of Illinois. The land there is
hilly, rolling in great waves. In fact, just a few miles away is the highest point in the state.

*By 7:45 A.M., Joel must be ready for the school bus. It will wind through six miles of
steep, gravel roads to bring him to the Scales Mound school, "Home of the Hornets."*

Above: *Joel does homework while his brother Bill eats a late supper after milking his dairy cows.* Below: *Joel and friends at his eighth-grade graduation party.*

Joel attends public school in Scales Mound in a split-level brick building with 235 other grade school and high school pupils. About half the students are farmers. This year Joel will graduate from eighth grade and begin ninth, but his class will not get larger. Except for three foster children who came and left, Joel has been with the same nineteen kids since first grade.

"I know every kid in practically the whole school," he says. "Some of those guys in schools like 'Welcome Back, Kotter' don't even know the people in their own class."

Joel is a good student, though reluctant to discuss it. "Yeah, I guess I pull mostly A's, some B's." In national testing Joel scored an overall 99 percent, meaning that only 1 percent of students scored higher. His studies are typical of any eighth grader's in the United States. "We're doing percents in math. English, forget it. In history we're up to F.D.R. In science we do experiments like taking this chemical HCl and blowing up pieces of chalk."

But when the school bus drops Joel off and he runs up the quarter-mile lane to his farmhouse, slips out of his sneakers, and pulls on his boots—then his life is no longer typical of an average teenager. His footgear is the clue. Joel wears boots every day, no matter what the season. That's because he does chores every night after school and for several hours on weekends. The chores are boot work—hard, heavy, and sometimes dirty.

*Joel heaves a wriggling, squealing, forty-five pound "escapee"
over the fence into the pig lot.*

Above: *Boots are indispensable to farm work.* Below: *Pigs instinctively nose out dirt or mud—wherever they may find it.*

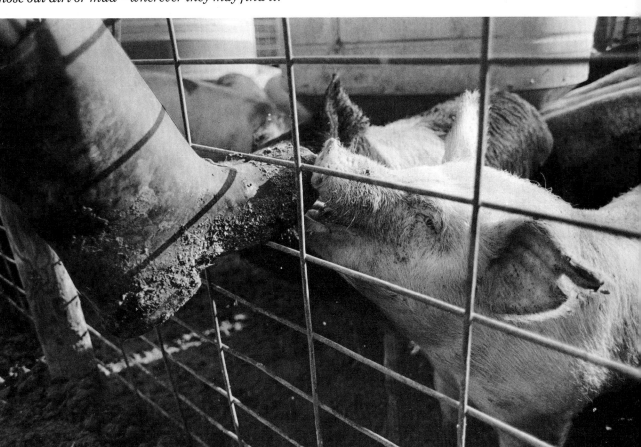

This bull pastures with twenty-five of Ed's beef cows.
Calves are born in spring and stay in the pasture with their mothers
until they're strong enough to join the rest of the herd.

The daily chores that Joel does help run the farm and help support the family. Joel is a teenager, but he does the work of a man. Unlike most families, where the parents alone make the money, farm families work together. Each child's labor is not only important to the family's well-being, it is essential.

The Hollands operate a self-sufficient farm, typical of many in the Corn Belt. They raise livestock—pigs, cattle, a few sheep. In each herd, they keep some females as mothers to replenish the stock. The rest of the animals are sold for slaughter, to become the pork, beef, and lamb on America's tables. The Hollands grow virtually all the food their animals need—corn, oats, and hay. They sell the surplus, though most of their money comes from selling the animals themselves.

To run a farm like this, a farmer has to have the skills of many men. He has to be a machine operator, driving immense and powerful vehicles; he has to be a mechanic, repairing them; a husbandman, raising livestock; a veterinarian, tending them when sick; an agriculturist, growing food on a large scale; and a businessman, managing (like Joel's father) a farm operation worth nearly one million dollars. As Joel works on the farm, he is all these men.

Yet he is a boy still and, like an apprentice, he continues to learn new skills. Joel takes his learning seriously because his goal is to become a farmer. He is extremely alert and watchful, like a cat. Even

Joel, Bill (center), and Terry (right) remove a barbed-wire fence.

when not actively involved in a chore, Joel can readily answer any question about what is going on. He listens as his dad counsels a seed customer in the kitchen, as his brother Terry consults a vet about recent deaths in his hog herd, as his older brothers discuss soil planning

Climbing the sixty-foot silo was a challenge Joel mastered this summer.

while they mend a fence. Knowledge seems to be constantly seeping, sometimes flowing, into Joel's mind.

Even before he could spell his name, Joel began learning about the farm, bumping along on a tractor seat between his dad's legs. He drove tractor himself in the fields when he was in second grade. By fifth grade he was driving farm machinery on public roads. He was doing hog chores by age seven, inoculating baby pigs by eleven, buying and feeding his own calves when he was twelve. Now, at thirteen, Joel is virtually head of a hog operation that grosses over forty thousand dollars a year.

Joel is the youngest of Ed and Betty Holland's six children. Only he and his brother Marty, sixteen, still live at home. Two other brothers, Bill, twenty-four, and Terry, twenty, come home each day to eat meals with the family. Bill and Terry rent neighboring farms. Each has his own livestock herd, but they farm their land collectively with their father.

Two other children, Kevin and Kathy, do not live at home. This year Kevin, twenty-two, will graduate from college in Chicago. He will be the fourth college graduate among the Holland children. "We insist they all go to college and get a taste of what it's like off the farm," says Betty. "Then if they want to come back to farming, fine."

Kathy, twenty-four, is the oldest child and the only daughter. She is now a Roman Catholic nun doing graduate study in Dubuque, Iowa. But, like her brothers, she grew up farming, and she still misses it. Kathy called this May during her final exams and said, "I'd give anything to be out plowing instead!"

As the youngest, Joel has at times had more farming "teachers" than he's wanted. One night he sat at the kitchen table listening to his dad and brothers talk about the rewards of farming.

Above: *Betty keeps the books for the farm operation, nearly a million-dollar business. The task requires her to spend eight hours a week at her desk.* Below: *Ed and Joel. "Joel's a lot like Dad," says Bill.*

Opposite: *Terry in the machine shed on his rented farm. He converted old disk plates to store nails, nuts, and bolts.* Above: *Marty bought his used Plymouth the day he got his driver's license.* Below: *Bill with one of his finest milkers.*

Joel throws hay for the sheep into the pickup. Basketball practice after school sometimes forces him to squeeze chores in late at night.

24

"It's a good, independent life," said Bill. "You're your own boss."

"I wouldn't know," said Joel, grinning. "I've got a boss."

"Who?" asked his dad.

Joel pointed to each one around the table.

Joel used to be largely at somebody's side, watching and listening, lending a hand, or going on the run for a tractor or forgotten tool. He took the occasional bossing he got in stride. Now, he is so busy with his own work that he is no longer available to be everybody's "go-fer."

Joel uses the front loader to dump corn into the sows' pasture.

Joel jumps from the cattle feeder after checking on the corn supply.

"If I had just one word to describe Joel, it would be *enthusiasm,*" says Betty. He uses his youthful energy indiscriminately. On one summer day, he jumped 15 fences, drove farm machinery 25 miles, fed 320 animals, opened and closed 8 gates, walked and ran about 8 miles, jumped on and off the tractor 26 times, lifted 900 pounds of grain, shoveled 4,000 pounds, and ate about 2600 calories!

A barbed-wire fence is the hardest of all to jump.

Cleaning out the oats "shed," actually a loft.

Time out.

Pigs like the mud, but Joel hates it.

On weekends and during the summer, Joel works outdoors any-
where from eight to fifteen hours a day. The only time he minds it is
during early spring. Then the snow melts and rain often pours down

Ankle boots are barely sufficient on a soggy day.

daily, turning the farmyard into a swamp. Muds sucks at his boots, making walking itself a tedious chore. More than the bother, though, Joel hates the ugliness. "When it rains, everything seems so awful."

Hunting deer after school with his dad.

Regardless of how much energy his work consumes, Joel has plenty left over for sports. He hunts deer and traps wildlife in the fall, and snowmobiles in the winter. Spring brings softball and basketball games, and summer provides weather for water-skiing and fishing. Nearly all his favorite sports are played outdoors.

A break from chores.

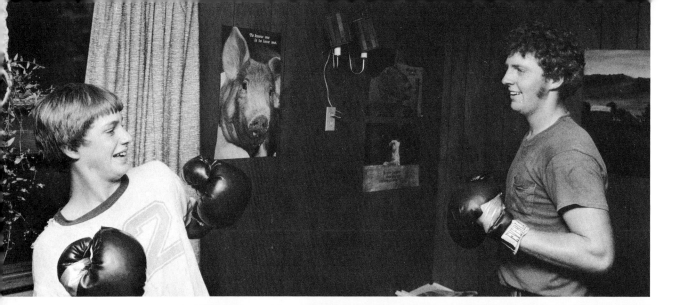

*Joel boxes with Terry in the family den, a room so mammoth
that it holds a Ping-Pong table, pool table, two couches, two coffee tables,
a piano, an organ, and three stuffed chairs.*

Water-skiing at a nearby lake.

The Holland front yard, 9:00 A.M.

If he had to live in the city for a year, Joel says he would mostly miss "the land. I'd miss seeing things grow. The change of seasons." In fact, if Joel could choose any place in the world to live, he guesses he'd live "right here. It'd have to be country. After living out here, I don't think

Joel hikes home through the west hayfield.

I'd ever want to be in the city. You just don't have the freedom. Or the responsibilities. I'm not saying a city kid doesn't have responsibilities. But you don't work as a family the way you do on a farm. It'd just have to be country for me."

WORKING WITH ANIMALS

Joel's brother Bill is a dairy farmer. He has to milk his cows before dawn. Each morning, Joel's brother Marty gets up at five o'clock to help Bill. The world is still black as pitch as Marty drives his old Ford two miles down the dusty gravel road to Bill's farm.

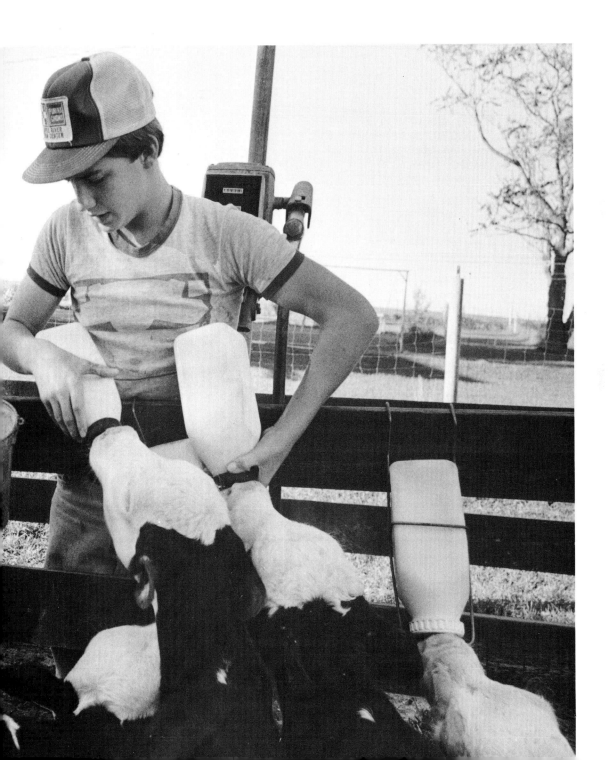

Back home, Joel is still in bed. He gets to sleep "late" until seven. "I'm not a morning person at all," he explains. "I don't really start going until about ten o'clock." During the fall and winter, Joel's folks wake him. "When Mom and Dad go downstairs they usually just shout in my room." But in the spring and summer, Joel has a unique alarm clock: the bellow of baby calves.

"They force me awake in the morning. They just yell and scream." The baby calves belong to Joel, and they bleat in the morning because they are hungry. A farmer is his own boss, yet work usually kicks him out of bed at an early hour.

All Joel's calves are male, born to dairy cows on Bill's farm. Bill keeps the female calves that are born and raises them to become milkers. During mild spring and summer months, he sells all the male calves to Joel for "about the going rate" ($125 now). When the weather becomes cold, he sells the males for veal, because Joel has no heated barn in which to shelter them.

The calves are just three days old when Joel brings them in the pickup truck to the old henhouse on his farm. (They leave their mothers when they are this young because Bill wants to sell as much of the mothers' milk as he can.) They will stay in the henhouse until they are about four weeks old and strong enough to graze on grass in the Holland yard.

The older calves race for Joel as he blinks his way into the bright sunlight carrying their bottles of milk replacement (water mixed with

These calves have just had their morning bottles. Smelling milk replacement on Joel's fingers, they follow him to the henhouse.

a powdered substance that contains all the nutrients of milk). If there are only two calves, Joel will give them their meals on the spot, holding the two-quart plastic bottles as the calves tug and suck. They empty the bottles in a minute, and then lick each others' mouths to get the last precious drops. As Joel goes to the henhouse to feed the

In the yard, Joel feeds his calves, four and six weeks old.
After bottle-feedings, calves lick each other's mouths for more drops of milk.

younger ones, the calves sometimes trot after him, trying to lick any drops of milk that happen to have spilled on his fingers.

When there are several calves to feed at once, Joel props the bottles on wire racks attached to a fence. The calves line up to eat, their necks outstretched to reach the hanging nipples. At about five o'clock in the afternoon, Joel feeds each calf another two-quart bottle.

Feeding the calves is a miniscule task compared to feeding the pigs and hogs. (Hogs are swine that weigh over 120 pounds; pigs weigh under that.) On Joel's farm, there are usually about 350 feeder pigs and hogs—swine being fattened for sale. And, as the saying goes, "they eat like pigs." The herd consumes about two tons of feed every three days!

Joel is the one who feeds them. In fact, he handles every aspect of their care. He has been in charge of the herd since his brother Terry left last year to rent his own farm. With the livelihood of the herd in his hands, Joel cannot take days to goof off and do nothing. His animals would go hungry. Perhaps one would get sick and need attention. Tending livestock every day kept Joel's parents from taking a vacation for nineteen years, until their sons were old enough to cover for them. Yet the responsibility does not seem to weigh on Joel. Having grown up around livestock, he is accustomed to their constant needs. He feeds them each day as routinely as he feeds himself.

Feeder pigs and hogs eat mainly shelled corn. Joel grinds corn for

Joel carries a seventy-five-pound pail of supplement feed to the mixer mill.

them in the mixer mill, a huge machine that towers ten feet above his head. Powered by a tractor, it grinds the corn as fine as powder and mixes it with supplement feed, which Joel dumps into a hopper at the side of the mill. "The supplement is the only feed we buy our animals," he explains. It contains mostly protein, and Joel varies the amount he puts into the mill according to the size of swine he is feeding. The swine live in three separate places, grouped by size, because the younger pigs need more protein than the older hogs.

45

The mixer mill grinds corn and shoots it up a long tube into a grain-O-vator, where it stays until it is needed to feed the cattle.

The mixer mill is as noisy as it is big, and it spits. As Joel stands beside it, making sure corn is flowing freely into the mill's other hopper, his face may get stung by flying bits of corn. On hot summer days, fine particles of ground corn stick to Joel's brow. Otherwise the job is more time-consuming than difficult.

Joel's father sometimes grinds the hog feed if he has an extra hour while Joel is in school. But more often the favor is reversed, and Joel helps his father by grinding feed for the cattle as well as the swine. (Joel's father takes care of the cattle herd, just as Joel looks after the hogs.) For the cattle, Joel grinds up ear corn. Unlike hogs, cattle can digest and utilize nutrients in the entire corn plant—kernels, cob,

The mixer mill doesn't do all the work. Joel sometimes has to shovel in all the corn—about two tons per load.

stalk, and all. Usually numbering about 125, the cattle consume the same amount of feed as the hogs—roughly four tons a week. Since the mixer mill has a two-ton capacity, Joel grinds four loads per week.

The job of grinding feed is routine for Joel, but that is what makes it dangerous. Repetition of a task can breed carelessness, and being careless with a powerful machine like the mill is a serious mistake. "A mill will take your arm off if you put it where you shouldn't," says Joel's father. Respect for the machine helps keep Joel cautious. He knows where every moving part is, and what it does. He always turns off the engine before he places his hand on a screen that conceals whirling, grinding blades beneath.

Joel empties about one-third of the grain-O-vator's load into the cattle's feed bunks.

48 At evening chore time, after Joel grinds the corn, he hauls the full mixer mill to the swine. Each of the three swine groups lives in a barn that has one side open to a fenced-in dirt lot. Two groups share the same barn and lot, the barn partitioned by a wooden wall, and the lot partitioned by a fence. In the lots are bins, and into the bins the long arm of the mill dumps its load. Except when they are being moved, the pigs and hogs spend their entire lives eating and sleeping, coming and going from barn to lot. They don't get particularly excited when they see food coming because they have been eating all day long. Joel never lets their self-feeding bins get completely empty.

One group of hogs, however, does get very excited when they hear the nightly chug-chug of Joel's tractor. They are the sows—the mother hogs. The sows live in an old hayfield next to the farm buildings and mostly feed themselves by grazing on the grass, clover, and alfalfa that grow there. (In winter, they stay in an open barn and are fed corn and oats.) An all-day corn diet like the feeder hogs have would make them too fat to deliver babies. They do, however, need some corn for additional nourishment. So every night at chore time Joel attaches a front loader (just a big scoop) to the tractor, fills it with corn, and drops it over the pasture fence. When the sows come running on their short, stubby legs and begin munching corn in a chorus of grunts and snorts, Joel takes a mental count. If a sow is missing, it is usually for one reason: she is giving birth, or getting ready to, in the pasture.

This sow nosed together a nest of loose hay for her newborn litter. Ed rings the sows' snouts so that the metal will jar the sensitive part if they try to root up entire plants.

Three times this year sows gave birth in the pasture. Once was this fall. By the time Joel bounced the pick-up truck through the sows' hayfield in search of the missing mother, she had already delivered a healthy litter of nine pigs. They lay asleep, pillowed against their mother's great warm belly, surrounded by a nest of weeds and alfalfa, which the sow had rooted up and packed together with her snout. If the weather had been colder, she would have nosed together a nest so large that she and her brood could burrow underneath it completely. Joel knew enough about a sow's protective nature to keep his distance. Nonetheless, she gave a snorting growl when she saw him, stationing her swelled body between him and her babies. Joel picked several ears of ripe corn for her from the adjacent field, placed them a few feet away, and quietly left the sow to her natural home.

Although the sow and her babies survived the dangers of the open field, the Hollands do not like the sows to give birth out there. "If we were to let the sows farrow [give birth] in the pasture, coyotes would eat half the babies," says Joel's dad. "They usually farrow near a stream, and the babies might go in there and drown. Nights are cold. They could get pneumonia."

"The real reason," Joel added later, "is that we can watch the babies if they're inside. And it's a real pain separating them from the sow out in the field when they have to be weaned." So, a few days before a sow is due to deliver, Joel brings her in the hog carrier—a metal pen attached to a tractor—to a small barn called the farrowing house. He

Joel hooks up the hog carrier to move sows from field to barn.
Cousin John, who visited this summer, helps.

knows approximately when the sows are due to deliver because he has
recorded the date he and his dad released the two boars (male hogs)
into the sow pasture. "Due date should be three months, three weeks,
and three days later." But nature is unpredictable. Not all sows will
get impregnated at once, and those that do may deliver early. The best
clue to a due date is the size of the sow and the size of her udder, which
begins to fill with milk a few days before delivery.

Joel is getting good at spotting the sows that are due. It is one of the

Overleaf: *The narrow confines of a farrowing crate keep a four-hundred-pound sow from moving around. The raised gate allows her babies to nurse.*

many important responsibilities which his father entrusts to him. A farmer has to make countless decisions each day, so independent thinking is an essential skill. Ed Holland has fostered it in his children by letting them make judgments on the farm, not simply help with the labor. When Ed has a suggestion, he almost always prefaces it with "Why don't you maybe..."

"Dad doesn't tell me what to do," says Joel. "He'll let me go so far, then stop me. Like the other day we had some sows to bring over [from pasture to farrowing house]. I brought some too early. Dad looked at them and said they wouldn't have pigs for a while. He didn't complain, though. He really doesn't have to do any of the work."

There is more work than usual when the sows farrow, which they do about three times a year. Then Joel spends a great deal of time in the farrowing house, a small barn that can seem slightly creepy at first. It is low and dark, like a cave. Stringy cobwebs, heavy with dust, drape the rafters. But the gloomy impression does not last. Pigs scamper about. Sows give birth, nurse. The feeling is almost cozy.

The sows give birth in farrowing crates, metal pens that line the left wall. A gate across the center of each crate separates a sow from her litter. Raised four inches off the floor, it allows the babies to scamper back and forth to nurse. At the same time it keeps the sow stationary and lessens the chance of her smothering a baby pig, an accident that sometimes happens in an open area where she can move around and suddenly plop her great bulk down on the brood scampering beneath her.

53

The sows stay with their litters in the crates until the pigs are two weeks old. Then they're all moved to the "nursery" along the right wall. It's a large pen that holds four or five sows and their newborn all at once. On the other half of the wall is a pen of four- to six-week-old pigs, which have been weaned; their mothers have gone back to pasture. The young pigs stay in the pen, learning to eat from self-feeding bins and to drink water. They need time to gain size before they leave the "nursery" and compete in the "real world" of the feeder-pig barn.

At evening chore time, Joel sends the sows out of the farrowing house to eat in a fenced-in area where he has dumped a special sow feed made mostly of oats, a high-energy food. This food is stored in a nearby barn, and Joel carries it to the sows in five-gallon buckets. Now he does it without strain, but in second grade, when he began helping his dad and brothers with chores, transporting them was a challenge. "I'd always try to go the whole way without stopping," he says. "I'd make myself keep going. Usually I'd have to stop once before I got there, though."

Joel opens the farrowing crates and gives each sow a get-going poke when it's time to eat. Most sows weigh 250 pounds, and some weigh as much as 450. But 115-pound Joel moves among them without fear. "Naw, they won't hurt you. You have to respect them though. They have their babies."

Sows never seem to be in a hurry, and Joel is patient with them. He learned a lesson two years ago about pushing one too far. "Back when

Piglets and sows in the nursery pen. Litters sleep together, but when it's time to nurse, each one seeks its own mother.

*Outside the farrowing house, Ed uses the loader
to dump manure into the spreader.*

we had the old wooden pens, I got an electric prodder from Terry for Christmas. A sow wouldn't get out of the farrowing crate. I decided I'd give her a little shock to get her going. She got up all right! She started coming toward me. I even left my electric prodder in there."

While the sows are feeding, Joel cleans the farrowing house. The sows "toilet train" themselves to the outdoors, but, of course, the baby

Manure—a natural fertilizer—will be spread over one-third of Ed's fields by the end of the year.

pigs are not trained. Joel shovels their manure into the alleyway, then scrapes it out the back door. Later, when the pile of manure is big and he has the time, he will help his dad and brothers scoop it up with the front loader and dump it in the fields. In this way, the land receives back some of the nutrients it relinquished to the crops that went to feed the sows.

Spreading the bedding. Joel has just moved a group of sows and their litters out of the nursery pen and is preparing to move a new group in.

Bad weather can intensify cleaning chores. On rainy days, the sows carry mud and muck into the farrowing house, which Joel has to shovel away. And in winter, he needs to remove dirty bedding—using a shovel in the small farrowing house, but a tractor and front loader in the other barns. Then he spreads fresh bedding—either straw or ground corncobs. It will keep the pigs warm. "Clean sheets," says Joel.

Whenever there are two-day-old pigs, Joel performs surgery after cleaning the farrowing house. "I do it when the sows are out," he says. "But if they hear a baby crying, they'll all come running in." That's

A wheelbarrow blocks an anxious sow while Joel operates.

Joel squirts iron serum into a pig's mouth.

why Joel operates inside a crate where a sow could not charge him. He picks up a pig from a litter, his hand gently encircling its small neck. Then he squirts iron serum into its mouth. Until recently, Joel injected the serum into a back leg with a needle and syringe. "It wasn't hard. After you've done things a few times, it gets to be real automatic. Terry just showed me there's a hind muscle back there. Hit them there and you'll be all right."

After squirting the serum, Joel cuts the pig's eight needle teeth—two on each side, top and bottom. Aptly named, these teeth are sharp and thin. With such weapons, the pigs could hurt one another badly, gouging and scraping each other's faces as they compete for space to nurse. Even without needle teeth, a pig's bite is powerful. "If pigs have nothing else to do, they'll chew on each other's tails," says Joel's father. "It's usually just one that starts it, but then all the rest may pounce right on the pig, biting and chewing. That's why we cut the tails off."

Joel cuts the tail right after the teeth. Holding the pig by a hind leg, he snips the tail with the cutters, leaving about a half-inch stub, and sprays the wound with disinfectant.

Then, with a tool that operates like a paper hole-puncher, Joel notches the pig's right ear: one notch for a male, two for a female. "One reason we ear-notch is for security," Joel explains. "Last year when hog prices were up, there was quite a rash of hog stealing. Let's say somebody takes a truckload of your pigs. If they're all uniformly

Above: *Joel works swiftly, so the pig's distress is only momentary.*
Below: *If left to grow, the tail would be curly and ten inches long.*

Two notches in the ear identify this curious creature as female.

notched, it's going to be tougher for them to get rid of the pigs. But by law the only real claim you have is if you brand. The other reason is it makes sorting easier when it's time for castrating."

Within thirty seconds, the entire operation is over and Joel releases the pig, which dashes over to hide its nose under a brother or sister's belly. He reaches for another one. By the end of a litter, Joel's hands are bloody. If he operates on twenty or more, his fingers may be cramped. Yet the procedure is almost automatic for him; he has done it for hundreds of pigs.

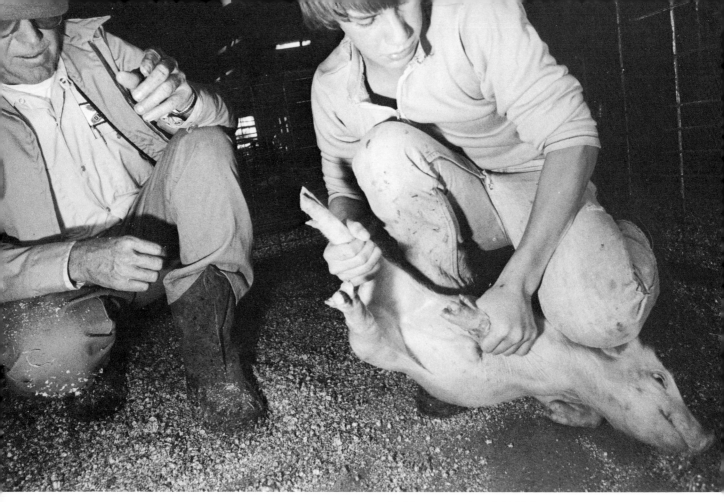

Joel braces a pig while Ed prepares to castrate.

Castration is another surgical procedure the male pigs endure before they leave the farrowing house. Joel explained why. "We castrate
so we don't have to worry about inbreeding and because they gain
quicker and the meat tastes better. Boar meat has quite an odor."

Joel does not castrate yet. But, like a nurse, he assists his dad. Joel's
main job is to hold the pig still so that his father's razor blade can
make swift, accurate incisions. The pigs are about five weeks old
when they're castrated. They weigh about twenty-five pounds by

then, and they use all their weight to try to wriggle free from Joel's grasp. He has to muscle a pig to the floor and pin its head with one knee and its hind end with the other. Then, with lightning-quick strokes, Ed does the cutting that will make the pig sterile. Joel sprays the wounds with disinfectant, and releases the frantic pig.

Mercifully, the operation is only seconds long, but it is painful and the patients fill the farrowing house with shrieks. Joel tries to ignore the pandemonium. He sees castrating as an essential part of raising pigs. "Yeah, it makes me feel bad," he says, "but it's gotta be done." The best way Joel can help the pigs is by holding them still. He and his dad schedule the operation for one week after weaning and one week before moving out of the farrowing house "so they don't have to go through all that stress at once."

Joel also receives veterinary experience at unscheduled times—when the animals become sick. Certain swine epidemics can spread from farm to farm the way measles may travel through a town. Because livestock live close together and eat from the same feeders, an animal with a contagious disease threatens the entire herd. If one or two of Joel's pig's fall ill, treatment must be immediate. Joel looks for signs of poor health each day. Loose manure is often the best indication. He also looks for strange behavior, such as a wobbly or listless pig. If he spots a sick animal, he tells his dad, who calls Doc Hepperly. Tom Hepperly is a young, bearded veterinarian, so kind-hearted that he keeps about his porch and yard all the stray dogs and cats that people bring him to "put to sleep."

If the livestock have an infection, Hepperly prescribes an antibiotic, and the Hollands administer it themselves. Doctoring is hard work, but it is satisfying. The medication is usually effective, and the animals recover. Nonetheless, some animals don't respond to treatment, and then the work is discouraging.

This summer one of Joel's calves had its knee stepped on by its mother shortly after birth. (The mother was a wild cow that Bill later sold.) The knee became infected and swelled to the size of a baseball, making the leg useless. Joel called Doc Hepperly, who cut the sore open to drain it and remove infected matter. He prescribed antibiotics.

At first, the calf could still walk.

And he suggested that Joel rig up a tire swing as a support to help the calf stand and walk to "work up muscle." Joel roped two inner tubes to rafters and placed the calf inside: front legs in front of one tire and back legs behind the other. Still, its legs buckled as soon as it tried to stand. Nothing worked. The calf died about two months later.

"I messed around with that calf all summer, and it died," said Joel, disheartened. A compassionate boy, he questioned whether he and the vet should have let the calf die of natural causes soon after birth. "I feel sorry for a calf like that. I sometimes wonder if we had left it alone how long it would've stuck around."

69

Joel and cousin John offer comfort while Doc Hepperly drains pus.

70   Doc Hepperly is one of the "regulars" who visit the Holland farm for business. The local truckers are regulars, too. They come about every two weeks, all year long, to haul the Holland hogs to market. "Bill has his milk check twice a month; we have the hog check," says Betty. "It pays the monthly bills."

Joel and his dad have the full-grown hogs ready to go by the time the truckers arrive, usually at nine o'clock in the morning. Joel begins the process at about eight o'clock at the barn where the largest feeder hogs live. Holding a red wax crayon, he walks among the hogs, weighing them with his eyes, watching for those that look as though they weigh between 220 and 230 pounds. When he spots a market-ready hog, Joel crayons a line down its back. "Dad's been letting me mark them now for two years," he says, proud of the responsibility. If he makes a mistake and misses a ripe hog, his dad will lose money at the next sale. "If a hog weighs over 230 pounds," Joel explains, "Dad gets docked 25¢ per 100 pounds." That's because the meat of a fat pig tastes tough.

When the marking's done, Joel and his dad drive any hogs that are in the feedlot into the barn to join the rest of the group, and they close off the exit with a portable panel gate. Out the side door of the barn is a fenced aisle. The truckers will back up against this aisle, let down a ramp, and herd the marked hogs out of the barn, down the aisle, and up the ramp to the truck. The unmarked hogs have to be out of the way when they come. So Joel and Ed sort them when all the hogs are

inside the barn; the marked ones stay, and the unmarked ones go out to the feedlot.

Ed stations himself by the panel gate while Joel heads unmarked hogs toward him. "S-s-s!" he says. "Yo! Let's go." Joel sometimes puts his hands on a hog's back to guide it toward the exit, but he doesn't rush the hogs. That would only make them frantic. Ed lets out the unmarked hogs, and quickly jabs the gate against marked hogs that try to get out.

The Hesselbacher clan (fathers, sons, nephews, and so on) usually haul Ed's livestock, and their wooden trucks almost always clatter up the lane just as the sorting is done. The Hesselbacher men are outgoing and friendly, and the Hollands look forward to seeing them. The men always talk about the weather and the price of hogs. And their conversations abound with stories of local news: how one guy's uncle had an invasion of army worms that stripped his cornfields as bare as a counter top; how another went to Missouri and saw fields so dry that a tractor engine would ignite them; how at a recent farm auction someone sold each of his dairy cows for a thousand dollars more than he paid for them.

Joel and Marty especially enjoy talking with David, thirty, who lives in the town of Scales Mound.

"How 'bout that?" said Dave one day when a truck was loaded with hogs in only three minutes. "That's how good we are."

Joel: "That's how good your help is."

"Ho!" said Dave.

The hogs run from the truck (parked outdoors) into the weighing pen.
The entire floor forms the platform of a scale. Joel takes a final look.

"That's one thing, Joel, you're modest," Marty ribbed.

Then, knowing that Joel, too, gets paid every market day, Dave said, "You have a good thing going here, Joel. You get the pigs free, the corn free. All profit."

Joel: "All but the trucking."

"We'll have to raise that, I can see," said Dave.

"Aw, you guys enjoy the scenery coming out here, don't you?" quipped Joel.

Dave: "Nothing to see but cornfields."

"That's more than you see in town, isn't it?" said Joel. "There's a spider on your pocket, Dave."

"Get down from there", said Dave, glancing at the creature clinging to his shirt. "He wants to drive to town with me. He don't like it out here."

Joel: "Probably wants to go to the tavern."

"Could be," agreed Dave.

When the hogs are all loaded and conversations finished, everyone leaves for the weighing station—the Hesselbachers hauling the hogs,

Joel waits as Popeye Hesselbacher writes out his hog check.

and Ed and Joel following behind in their own truck. After the hogs are weighed Popeye Hesselbacher writes out a check for Ed. The Hesselbachers are livestock dealers as well as truckers. They buy hogs from area farmers, then sell them to a large packing company forty miles away in Dubuque, Iowa. At Ed's request, Joel, too, receives a check. He is paid two dollars for each hog that is sold and the amount is deducted from Ed's check.

Joel takes his earnings seriously. Once, when Popeye shorted him two dollars, Joel lightly chided at the next sale, "Hey, don't be ripping me off this time!"

Joel also earns money on the calves that he raises. Next year, when the sixteen calves Joel raised this year are sold as full-grown cattle, he will probably receive about five thousand dollars.

What does he do with his money? "I put it in the bank. I have nothing to buy, really."

Many farm children do not make as much money. But Joel's parents believe that the children should share in the profits because they work to make them. Also, they realize that making money keeps Joel alert—if he loses a pig or calf, the money comes out of his pocket.

Making money on the animals is the final goal of livestock farming. Joel does not ponder the animals' butchered end anymore than most people do who eat their meat, nor has he ever witnessed it at a packing plant. His concern is with the many living animals on the farm—to shelter, feed, and care for them there. He tends them, but he does

Lamby, Joel's orphan pet, bleats at the back door for her bottle.

not become attached to the older livestock. Farm children grow up knowing animals are raised for food, not fun.

Yet Joel does make pets of some baby animals. He has a nurturing streak that lets him enjoy the dependence of the babies, and for years he has been adopting them. Once, when he was six years old, he took care of a lamb whose mother had died. Joel named the orphan Boobelee. Like a puppy, Boobelee would wait for Joel on the porch and trot after him about the farm. When Joel weaned him, Boobelee joined the other sheep, though he continued to be tamer then the rest of the

Above: *One of Joel's calves with Jessi.* Below: *Jessi's leg
was broken when she ran at a tractor Joel's cousin John was driving.
This cast replaces another, which she chewed off.*

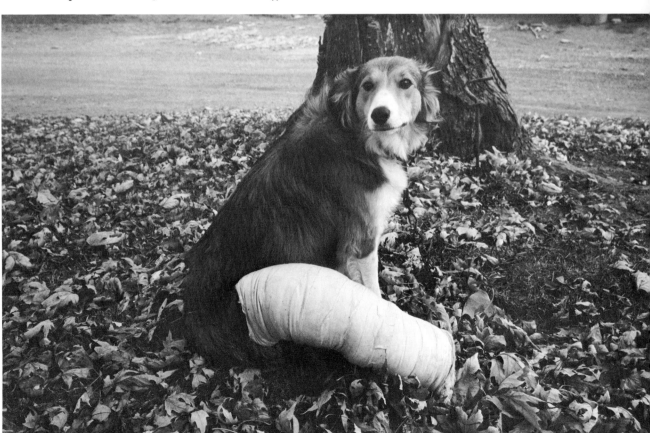

skittish flock. A year later, Boobelee was ready for market. Again his enchanted luck interceded: a farmer bought him to be the ram for his herd of ewes. Boobelee was Joel's first experience with selling an animal he had befriended as a baby, and he hadn't yet developed an indifference toward sending them off to market. His dad said Joel "felt real good" when Boobelee became a breeder instead of lamb chops.

Even now, Joel treats his baby calves like pets. But his attachment disappears as they join the herd, grow, and live in a pasture where he rarely sees them. When the steers are sold, the experience is not difficult for Joel.

Cleaning the farrowing house on a hot day. The Fly Zapper is overhead.

Facing an animal's death on the farm, however, is troubling to him. This summer he experienced it.

It was July when a scorching heat wave settled on most of the country, including Scales Mound. The excessive heat made Joel's cleaning chores in the farrowing house extremely unpleasant. Sweat poured off his arms as he shoveled manure out of the farrowing crates into the aisle. Normally pungent smells were now putrid. One hot day, Joel's brother Bill mentioned how the sun made farm work much harder. He had been driving tractor in the fields to weed the corn. "That ain't work," said Joel. "You should've been cleaning farrowing crates."

A bushel of dead flies.

Hogs try to escape the sun's blast in the shade of their open barn.

On Joel's farm, the enormous sows suffered most from the blistering temperatures, which reached one hundred degrees day after day. They lay for hours each day, motionless except for the twitching of their ears to shoo flies. Sows in the pasture wallowed in streams for relief. In the sow yard beside the farrowing house, they drooped under a cool

A stream in the farrowing house yard provides relief from the heat.

stream of water that Joel turned on to help them escape the sun's torment. Sows, like all hogs, are particularly susceptible to high temperatures because they cannot sweat to cool off. The sweltering heat trapped inside their huge bodies causes fevers that can result in heatstroke and death.

82   The close quarters of the farrowing crates were especially stuffy, so during the blazing afternoons Joel let the sows out onto the farrowing house aisle, where they received air, however stale, from open doors on either side. To diminish the hordes of flies inside the farrowing house, he rigged up an electric gadget, which emitted a shock to kill any fly that trespassed on its exposed wires. "I don't know what they call it in the book. I call it a Fly Zapper," he said. "It really fries those flies." The *zzt zzt* of the zapper was almost constant during the heat spell. Each week Joel emptied nearly a bushel of dead flies, pouring them into the manure pile like cereal from a box.

One Monday evening in the middle of the heat wave, Joel was sending the sows out to the lot to feed. One sow would not move. Just hours earlier she had delivered a litter of twelve healthy pigs. Now she lay in the aisle, her enormous sides heaving, careless of Joel's pokes. Something was wrong. Joel began to splash her back with cool water from a nearby trough. Finally the sow heaved up her great weight and went out to eat.

The next morning when Joel went to the farrowing house, already an inferno by eight o'clock, he found her stiff. He didn't glance then at the babies near her side. He knew several of them must be dead, too, from starvation. Joel left right away to find his dad, who was just coming out of the house. "Dad, you know that sow that had twelve pigs yesterday? She's dead."

"Heatstroke, I imagine," said Ed matter-of-factly. Throughout the

Joel searches the litter for signs of life.

entire ordeal of disposing of the dead sow and her babies, Ed would
remain businesslike and efficient. He had encountered death before.
So had Joel, but not often enough to accept it with nonchalance.

Ed went to get Terry for more help, and Joel returned to the farrowing house. He leaned heavily against the gate of the farrowing crate
and searched the dead sow's litter for signs of life. When he spotted
any feeble movement, he picked up the pig and squirted cow's milk
into its mouth. Six pigs had already died.

Ed, Joel, and Terry strain to pull the sow out of the farrowing house.

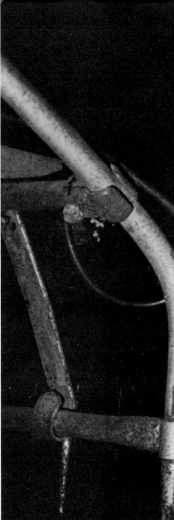

Rendering works will pick up the sow by noon.

Ed and Terry came in and tied a rope to the sow's front legs. Together with Joel, they dragged the 450-pound sow out of the narrow crate. One pig escaped under the gate and scampered frantically about its mother, nosing her cold body and looking for a nipple to nurse. Joel fetched the tractor, and with a chain attached to the rope, pulled the sow the rest of the way out of the hog house.

Joel places a dead pig into a feed sack

"Mama's leaving, little pig," said Ed.

Then Joel came back to dispose of the dead pigs in a feed sack, which he placed outside by the sow. The rendering truck would haul them all away by noon. "What a way to start a morning, huh?" he said, grimly. "The worst part is the pigs. They probably won't make it." None of the pigs in the litter did survive.

In all, the heat wave stole the lives of one boar and four sows. (Three had not yet farrowed when they died.) Joel began conditioning his response to be more like his father's. When asked about the death a few days later, he said casually, "Oh, you have to expect that raising livestock. It's all part of the business." Indeed it is. Birth and death are continuous cycles on a farm. A farmer is their first-hand witness. It is the births, which occur hundreds of times more frequently, that salve the bite of loss.

A sow may take from twenty minutes to two hours to give birth. Usually she will deliver in the dark and quiet of night, and Joel will not be there. But sometimes he will enter the farrowing house in the middle of a birth. If it is winter, he places a heat lamp above the huddling piglets, no bigger than hamsters. Then he leaves the sow to the privacy and efficiency of her own instincts.

The birth of a calf is not always so smooth. Unlike a sow, whose small offspring slip out easily, a cow gives birth to one large calf and frequently needs human assistance to deliver it. Ed's cows deliver in April; Bill's dairy cows deliver throughout the year. About one out of three in each group requires help. Joel has assisted at about fifteen births, but he "hasn't run the whole show yet."

Helping a cow deliver her calf is a strenuous job, usually involving two people. When Joel helps, he pulls up the cow's heavy, cumbersome tail to keep it out of the way and to steady her. The other person operates the puller, a contraption that helps tug the calf from its mother.

A newborn litter huddles under the heat lamp. Their protective mother gives the baleful eye.

This calf is being born in the normal "diving" position: head and front legs first.

90   The person cranking the puller strains with all his might to force a calf weighing sixty pounds out of a small opening.

The birth of a calf can sometimes be traumatic. Ed's pasture cows are wild, and simply corralling one that is calving is difficult. The task once "sent Terry right over the fence" when a cow charged him. The most tension is experienced by Bill, however. Dairy cows are worth more money than beef cows, because they produce saleable milk. The loss of one is a financial blow to a young farmer already

As Bill ties twine to the calf's hoof, Joel pulls so the calf won't slip back inside.

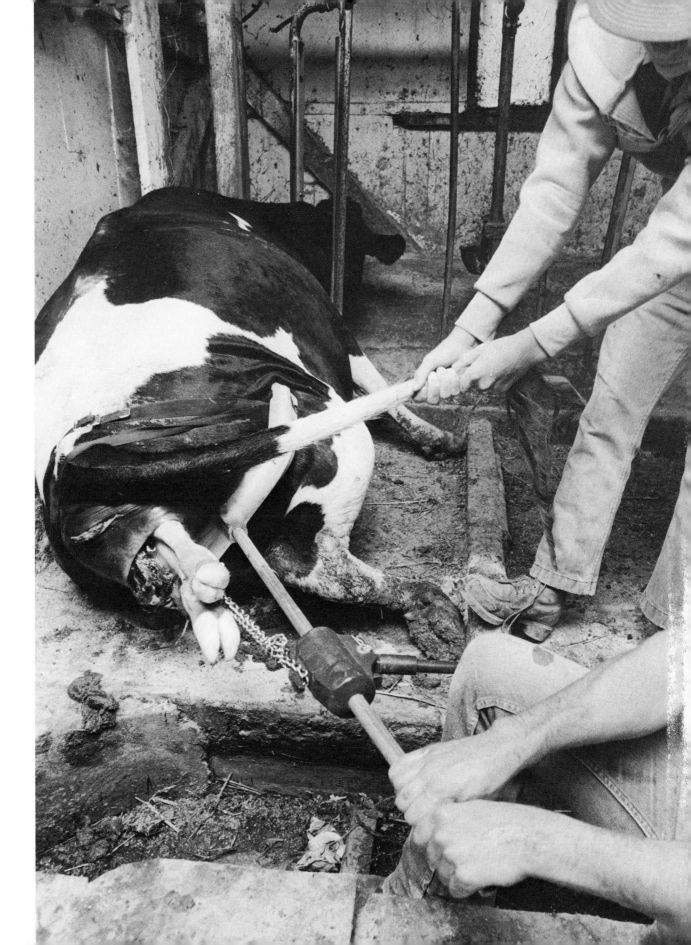

The ordeal is over. Bill helps the healthy newborn to stand.

heavily in debt. Some calving experiences are stressful enough to be fatal to the mother—a possibility that keeps Bill on edge until a birth is over and both cow and calf are healthy.

This spring, Joel helped Bill at a difficult delivery. Bill was nervous, and Joel became jittery trying to help. He was unsure of himself because he rarely assists Bill; Marty usually does. But with Joel yanking up on the cow's tail and Bill straining to wind the puller, they successfully delivered a healthy heiffer, a young female calf that would join the dairy herd in two years.

How did it feel for Joel to help? "It's neat, you know. You just brought a new life into the world," he said. Then, not wanting to appear too sentimental, he laughed, but his pride was genuine.

As Joel drove back home that spring morning after helping Bill, he was tired but relieved. The excitable sheep, grazing along the lane, ran away from his approaching pickup. Lamby was with them, an accepted member of the group since Joel had weaned her from a bottle a month ago. When he parked, the sheep huddled together for a while, then went back to munching weeds along a yard fence. Their propensity to eat weeds and grass difficult to reach with a lawn mower is the main reason the Hollands keep them. The sheep do what they please. No one bothers them except the pup, Jessica, when she is frisky and wants to watch them scatter. Otherwise, the sheep meander about the yard all day, seeking shelter in their half of the hog barn, its door always ajar.

Joel and Jess. A week before, playful Jess pulled Joel's boots
off the steps into the rain.

Joel slammed the truck door and Jessica ran up to greet him, flopping on her back and thumping her tail until he rubbed her belly. She followed Joel up the sidewalk toward the house. Under the maple tree's shady side rested three of his calves. In the farrowing house were over 100 pigs—some sleeping, others nursing. Joel could hear the bang-bang of the pigs' self-feeder lids coming from their various feedlots.

At the house steps, Joel stopped and kicked off his boots. He thought of the sow in the farrowing house who looked this morning like she was ready to deliver. Perhaps she had by now. He'd check on her after he grabbed a cookie inside and told his mom about the birth. In less than two minutes he would be pulling his boots back on.

FIELD WORK

Joel said, "I remember the first time I drove tractor. I was in second or third grade. I'd probably driven one with dad before, but that day they needed someone to drive the square-baler. I can still remember Dad told me to go right along the windrow, and if I got mixed-up or

*Farm machinery is parked indoors every night. Scales Mound is almost
free of serious crime, and keys are left in the ignitions of seventy-
thousand-dollar machines.*

something, to press the kill button, and I think I only had to press it
one time—when I started going off the windrow. It was a big tractor
then, too. I was really in the sky."

Joel no longer needs to concentrate so intensely as he did that hot
summer day when the tractor seat was adjusted down a foot so his
short legs could reach the pedals. Little by little, Joel gained experience driving a tractor, and by fifth grade he was one of the regular
field hands. Though some of the thrill has lessened, Joel still loves
field work. It is his favorite of all farm chores.

At first most of Joel's tractor experience was on the public road, not
in the field, driving to a 110-acre farm that his father owns on the
edge of Scales Mound, five miles from the home farm. Ed grazes a
herd of cows and their calves in a hayfield there. Joel was in fourth
grade then. "Every three days we had to go to the Uptown farm to
grind feed, and we had to pull the feed mill behind the tractor. Nobody
else wanted to drive it. You know, if somebody else would do it, they'd
let 'em. So I'd just drive the tractor and mill up there. I really learned
that road."

Gravel crunched beneath the tractor tires as Joel traveled the wind-
ing, hilly road. For years, one of the steepest hills enroute has been
known as Holland Hill. "Back in the old days," says Joel's father,
"when people wanted to know how good a car they had, they brought
it up Holland Hill. If it could make it up there in third gear, they knew
they had a good one."

Joel hooks up the manure spreader to the tractor's power system (PTO).

Joel had to downshift to sixth gear when his tractor panted up those inclines. But otherwise, he shoved into eighth gear and "raced" along at the tractor's highest speed—eighteen miles an hour!

Those early trips to the Uptown farm gave Joel the feel of a tractor—the bounce of its seat, the roar of its motor, the action of the steering wheel. He learned the basics of driving: how and when to shift to one of the eight forward gears and three reverse gears; how to keep a steady pace; how to drive straight. They were important skills, and yet driving in the field requires much more. Out there, a farmer does not simply drive a tractor, he operates it.

Except for the combine, which is self-propelled, a tractor pulls and powers every machine used in field work. Joel can operate nearly every machine on the Holland farm. This year he pulled twelve. Each one—attached in front of or behind the tractor—did a different job.

"It's different from driving on the road," he says. "You go slower, obviously. If you have an implement that's PTO-driven [that is, an implement whose moving parts are hooked up to the tractor's power system, called the *power take-off*], you have to keep the PTO up to 540 rpm's [revolutions per minute]. You have to watch that everything's working back there. A lot of it is experience. You can just tell if something is wrong."

Other Hollands also talk about tractor-driving as a sixth sense. "After you get used to a tractor, you can feel it in the tips of your fingers—how the engine's running, how the hydraulic system's going, how it's pulling by the sound of the motor," says Joel's dad.

"It's a deep mental thing," Bill explains. "You know how deep your chisel plow is just by the sound of the engine. You're on the tractor so long, if something is wrong you can feel that, just by a vibration." Experience teaches the features of the land and the quirks of the soil. "If someone just chisel-plowed and you're disking behind him, the soil will pull a little different," says Bill. Experience also teaches difficult maneuvers—like backing up a tractor and wagon to park them in a barn. "You steer your front end opposite where you want your back end to go. Then you have to compensate," Bill once tried to explain.

Farmers have their own gas pumps because their machines use so much fuel. The big tractors hold thirty-four gallons, but this "popper" only holds twelve.

"It's experience. When you have two or three loads of hay to back into the machine shed, and a storm is coming, you learn in a hurry." He paused and added, "The only way you really learn is go and bang up some machinery."

The Hollands' machinery is no longer banged up from learning mistakes, yet one machine or another is usually in need of repair, simply from regular use. The machines have thousands of moving parts, any one of which can break; and they have about three hundred tires, any one of which can go flat.

Before they can patch the tractor tire, Terry and Marty must find the tiny hole that's causing a leak.

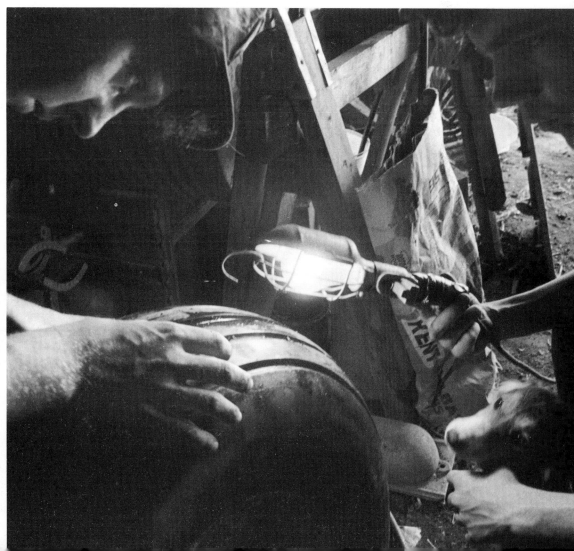

Joel helps Terry tighten a chain on the hay elevator,
which loosened after several hours of work.

104 When repairs are necessary, Terry makes them. He is the prime mechanic in the family, and his work saves the Hollands thousands of dollars each year. "If you bring a machine in [to a professional garage], they'll put two guys to work on it at twenty-one dollars an hour each," explains Ed. Joel often assists Terry, but he rarely fixes anything on his own. "I guess I could if I had to, but I don't have to yet."

In spare summer moments, Terry and Joel fix the elevator
that carries hay up to a loft.

A fifty-two-foot-long piece of the grain auger, which lifts corn into the drying bin, lies on the ground. Terry will repair it.

Joel gingerly removes oats that plug the combine.

*Inside the round baler, Joel watches Ed fasten the ends
of a new belt together.*

If a machine isn't needed right away, the Hollands will wait to repair it until they have some spare moments. But often, repairs have to be made on the spot. This summer, for example, a belt snapped on the round-baler Ed was driving. Since Ed always carried an extra belt with him, he signaled Joel, who was raking hay in an adjacent field, to come and help. Joel squatted inside the machine in the hollow space where the round bale is packed, and he and his dad threaded the belt in and around the machine parts, handing it back and forth to one another until all forty-seven feet of it were in place.

It is no surprise that the Holland machinery gets a hard workout. Counting the land that Terry and Bill rent, and the land that Ed owns, the Hollands farm one thousand acres. During seasons of field work, the machines toil across each acre several times.

Winter is the idle season in the fields. The ground, frozen to a depth of three feet, rejects any implement that tries to penetrate it. But every other season brings the farmer into the field: in spring to prepare the land and to plant; in summer to make hay; in fall to harvest.

More trips are made over the same ground in spring than at any other time. Planting the corn is one trip, one that Joel doesn't yet participate in. Only Ed (the most experienced) and Terry (the mechanic) run the planter. This complex machine not only buries seed in the ground, it deposits fertilizer and insecticide as well.

Before planting, however, several trips must be made to ready the soil for seed. At the start of spring, cornfields are littered with stalks from last year's crop. They have to be chopped and then blended in the ground. The soil itself, hard and caked in early spring, has to be made as fine as coffee grounds, so that new young roots can penetrate it deeply and so that nourishing rain can seep through. To accomplish this, the Hollands traverse each field with plows and disks that have a variety of claws, teeth, nails, and plates, which trample the trash and

The blades on the disk have to be sharp as knives to cut through the tough cornstalk fibers.

loosen the soil. Joel can drive all these spring machines except the chisel plow—a machine that his brother Bill bought this year. It's like a new toy, and all the Hollands want to operate it. "There isn't room for me to get in yet," Joel explains. This spring, he spent most of his time running the disk—an implement that chops up cornstalks with rows of metal plates.

In the spring, miles of earth in the Midwest are brown and bare. Corn seed is planted in the "valleys"; fertilizer is on the "peaks."

112
After the corn is planted and has grown about six inches high, the last spring trip is made. The machine used then is a cultivator—an implement with diamond-shaped hooks, which dig into the soil between the cornrows and uproot weeds.

On field-work days, Joel spends many hours on the tractor. Some people find this kind of work physically taxing. They complain of sore necks from constantly looking back and forth between the implement being pulled behind and the land coming up ahead. Some people's arms ache from remaining outstretched all day. Others dislike the long hours in the hot sun, or the snapping wind that turns their faces the color of rust. But Joel claims he's never stiff, sore, or tired after a day in the fields. "Young muscles, I guess."

The part of his body that tires most on a tractor is his ears! From a distance, field work looks tranquil. Joel's emerald green tractor glides over miles of soft, rolling land. But up close, the scene is not so mellow. The straining engine roars, sputters, and crackles. Above its blare, Joel blasts the radio, always tuned to rock music. "I think the noise when you're out on an open tractor makes the biggest difference when you get off," says Joel. "When you stop the tractor, everything is dead. You can hear a pin drop, you know. You can still hear that engine sound, though. I guess it gives some people a headache. I've never really had the problem. It's music really—especially the diesel sound of the big tractors."

114   The big tractors are the ones Joel loves to drive, but so does everyone else on the Holland team. Because Joel has least seniority, he usually drives a smaller one. This spring while the Hollands were cultivating, Joel was stuck on the smallest tractor, pulling the smallest cultivator. "I'd never want to drive that little popper in anything over a fifteen- or twenty-acre field because that's enough to drive you bonkers," said Joel. "You're only taking two rows every time you go around. I always think if I had a four-row, I'd be getting twice as much work done."

Seeing the clear results of his labor is part of what Joel enjoys about field work. Does he ever get bored going around and around the same field? "No. You can see something getting accomplished," he says. "That's enough for me, I guess." In summer, Joel was bouncing on the seat of a tractor for fifty hours or more a week to put up hay. He still insisted the work was not tedious. "You can go out on the farm the next day, say, and you've got this field of hay that you put up yesterday that's completely done, and then you move to the next field. Pretty soon you're done with one whole crop of hay."

Weather cooperating, the Hollands harvest three crops of hay in all: the first crop in late spring, the second and third crops in summer. Hay can be harvested more than once because it grows continually, like a lawn. Alfalfa, clover, and grass grow in the Holland's hayfields. The Hollands plant the alfalfa; the clover and grass grow wild. Four or five years after planting, the alfalfa crop is thin, so the hayfield must

Joel leaves the windows of his cab open as he rakes hay on a hot, humid day. An air-conditioned cab would allow him to "farm like a tourist," says Ed.

be plowed under and replanted. But for one year before replanting, the field is used as a pasture for sows and cattle. They wander through it all day, feeding on the plants. In the winter, snow buries and frost kills the all-day pasture meal of these livestock. Then they are fed hay. Baled hay is simply bundled pasture.

Joel travels across a hayfield three times, pulling a different imple-

The hay rake combs the cut hay into neat rows, called windrows. The tractor pulling this rake has done field work for over eight thousand hours.

ment behind his tractor each trip. First, he mows the hay, cutting it like lawn. Then he rakes it, piling the hay into windrows (neat lines). And finally he bales it, wrapping the hay into bundles. On many haying days, all the Holland tractors are in use. Baling alone requires four tractors: two to make and haul the round bales; two others to make and haul the square bales.

*Joel drives the bale-mover at about ten miles per hour. If faster, the
bulky, fifteen-hundred-pound bale may topple off.*

Joel cannot yet drive the machine that makes the round bales. It is complex, and he is needed anyway to help out with other haying stages. But he does drive the bale-mover, which picks up the round bales and hauls them, one at a time, to their destination. The bale-mover looks like a gigantic needle sticking out behind the tractor. Joel backs the needle into the center of a bale, pulls a lever that tilts it up, and rides away. Shaped like giant loaves of bread, the round bales stay outdoors all year, stacked in fields near the winter homes of sows and cattle. They are moved as needed to feed these livestock, whose hardy hides allow them to eat outdoors even during freezing weather.

Bill's dairy cows, on the other hand, stay indoors all winter, because they cannot tolerate frigid temperatures. Hay that will be fed to them is square-baled so that it can be hand-carried indoors. Hay is also square-baled when the Hollands plan to sell it or save it. The square bales are much smaller than the round bales and can easily be loaded into trucks or stored away in barns.

Whereas round-baling is a two-person job, square-baling requires a crew of four. Even Betty is sometimes a part of it. Although she has little confidence in her driving skills, she operates the tractor that pulls the square-baler and a flatbed wagon behind. "You know they're at the bottom of the barrel or I wouldn't be here." she laughs. "They tell me what gear, I shove it in, and away we go. I spend more time praying than anything else when I'm on the tractor!"

Joel throws the bales onto the hay elevator, which carries them to the loft where Marty waits.

Betty constantly looks down at the front right wheel to make sure it is running alongside the windrow. Meanwhile, the square-baler sweeps up raked hay, packs it into square bales, ties it twice lengthwise with twine, and shoots it out the back where another crew member (usually Ed) loads it onto a flatbed wagon.

Someone has to get the baled hay out of the field and into the loft. That's where Joel and Marty come in. Joel hooks up the loaded flatbed to a tractor and drives it to the barn. There he heaves the sixty-pound

Square baling. Betty prays and drives; Ed lifts and loads.

The spiky hay can cut skin.

bales onto a mechanical arm (called an elevator), which carries them up to the window of the hayloft. The work is scratchy, dusty, and dirty. Shreds of hay fly each time Joel picks up a bale; more fly out as the bale lands. Heavy gloves and work jeans help protect him from the coarse hay, which easily cuts bare skin.

The bales he throws have to land exactly in between the grooves of

Each bale weighs sixty pounds.

the elevator or they will not ride safely to the top. If Joel misses (about three times in a load of seventy to eighty bales), he jumps onto the bale to settle it in place. Otherwise, he keeps up a quick, steady rhythm, throwing a bale every five seconds. On a typical square-baling day, when the Hollands put up eight loads of hay, Joel lifts and throws over sixteen tons.

On a typical square-baling day,
Joel lifts and throws sixteen tons.

Adjusting the way one landed.

Joel drives the chopper, which prepares the hay that will be stored in Terry's silos (background). He must look back to make sure the hay is blowing into the wagon, and then look ahead to make sure the tractor drives along the windrow.

Inside the hayloft, Marty stacks the bales from floor to ceiling. Then the boys deliver the empty flatbed to Betty and Ed, just as another flatbed is full. The whole cycle takes about thirty minutes.

A lot of this labor would be saved if Ed had silos on his farm. Ed has always believed that a silo was not worth the fifteen-thousand dollar investment it would require, since he had six children to help him. But the man from whom Terry rents his land had only one daughter, so he bought silos. They greatly reduce a farmer's labor; baling is not necessary and feeding livestock is easier. All Terry has to do is push a button and the silage (hay that has fermented in a silo) is carried by a conveyor to his feed bunks. Silos also save precious time during haying because they can accept green juicy plants. Hay cut for silos does not have to dry two days in the sun, as it does when it is going to be baled.

This summer Joel learned how to drive a chopper, the machine that prepares Terry's hay for the silos. "Dad taught me how. He told me how fast to run it, what gear to put it in. We made a patch up and down the field. Just a matter of minutes."

The chopper cuts hay into pieces the size of toothpicks and shoots them up a tube into a wagon. The driver has to operate a crank, which aims the gush of hay. Working it can be tricky. "Dad told me when you go around a corner you crank twice so you don't lose any hay," says Joel. "That took a little learning. The first couple corners I cranked the wrong way." Did he lose any of Terry's hay? "Well, it wasn't anything to have a lawsuit over, you know."

The last crop of hay is usually put up in late summer. Then no more field work is done until harvest. It's hard for the Hollands to wait for harvest, because in a way they have been waiting since the corn was planted. Throughout the summer, farmers have a consciousness of

In mid-July, the cornstalks are already seven feet high,

and a concern for the growing corn. Its health seems to set the mood for the whole community. At the height of the heat wave this summer, Joel was asked how he liked the weather. The crop was his first thought. "Makes the corn grow."

though ears and kernels will not appear until August.

In preparation for harvest, Joel helps Ed and Marty clean out the empty steel shed. It will hold twenty thousand bushels of corn.

By September, the last of the corn was gone from the steel storage shed, and Joel helped his dad and Marty clean its floor. They swept away the fine red corn dust and other debris. "We should put a basketball hoop up in here," Joel remarked as he looked around the barren building. But then he reconsidered. Come harvest, the shed would once again closet twenty thousand bushels of corn.

By September, too, the corn leaves in the fields had dried from lush green to sandy brown. They crackled in the wind. Still, the ear of corn on each wizened stalk was not yet dry enough to pick. The Hollands wait for their corn to reach 25 percent moisture before they pick it. "Otherwise it will mush up in the combine from having too much water," explained Joel. When autumn winds begin blowing and the musty smell of harvest weather fills the air, the Hollands await that percentage impatiently. This year, the corn dried to 25 percent moisture on October 8, releasing the eager troops into the fields.

Harvest work is intense. Farmers race against approaching freeze and possible rain, both of which can halt field work. Each dry day they work well into dark. The lights of combine or tractor bounce across Midwestern cornfields long after the moon is up. "Our tractor might get started at four-thirty in the morning and won't get shut off 'till eleven at night," says Terry.

During this year's harvest, Joel jumped on any available tractor after school and basketball practice, and worked until ten o'clock. On weekends he worked a sixteen-hour day, like the others. Far from disliking the pace, Joel shared the infectious harvest enthusiasm of farmers finally reaping the year's labors. "I enjoy work in the fall more than anything, I guess," he said. "Things are going fast and everybody's moving. You know, everybody's out there in the fields—the neighbors are doing it, you're doing it. Everybody's going like mad."

Most of Joel's time this harvest was spent hauling picked corn from the field to its storage place. When he hauled shelled corn, Joel pulled an empty wagon to the cornfield and waited until the combine operator radioed "ready" on his CB. Then he drove the wagon directly under the spout of the combine, and 130 bushels of corn, yellow as a school bus, streamed into his wagon. "You can really feel the weight," he said, taking off with a six-ton load. Going down a small incline in the road he explained, "I'm idling now," but the weight of the corn pushed him as wind does a sailboat.

Joel and Marty haul corn, which the combine has picked and shelled.

The grain elevator carries corn fifty-three feet up to the top of the drying bin.

Ed doesn't have a silo, which can accept corn with moisture, so his corn has to be dried in a bin before it can be stored. Otherwise it will rot. An enormous fan under the raised screened floor of the drying bin dries five thousand bushels of corn at one time, bringing its moisture content down from 25 to 15 percent. To this bin, located twenty yards south of his home, Joel hauls each load of shelled corn. A grain elevator reaches from the ground to a hole at the top of the bin, waiting to carry the corn up. He parks the wagon so that its window is just above the elevator base. When he slides open the window, corn rushes into the elevator.

134   Then Joel drives the empty rattling wagon back to the field again. Enroute, he usually crosses paths with a second hauler who is carrying a full load. Together the haulers keep the combine operating without interruption.

This was the first harvest that the Hollands owned a self-propelled combine, a cavernous machine that lumbers through a cornfield gulping hundreds of cornstalks a minute, tearing off their ears, and scraping them clean. In previous years, Ed owned a picker-sheller, which was pulled and powered by a tractor. It picked only two rows at a time; the combine picks four. The older Hollands—Ed, Bill, and Terry—usually operate the combine. Especially Ed. "We can't get him off it," laughs Joel. "I don't blame him. After all those years with a two-row, and before that it was a one-row."

And, of course, before that it was by hand. Chick, the man from whom Terry rents his farm, told Terry about harvest thirty-five years ago. "Chick said that the horse would pull the wagon and the farmers'd pick," recalls Terry. "If he was lucky, he got one load of corn in the morning and one load in the afternoon, picking it by hand. There'd be 40 bushels a load, so 80 bushels a day." This harvest, the combine readies three or four *thousand* bushels of corn in a good day. Most acres yield 140 to 150 bushels.

Now and then, more for a treat than anything, Joel gets a turn driving the combine. He sits near the edge of the seat as he maneuvers the monstrous machine, looking *down* on cornstalks that are six feet tall. "You get a feeling of power up there in the cab," says Joel. "It's big."

Joel operates the combine at 10 P.M.

It is also complex. A series of controls sprays across the panel in front of the operator. Joel does not touch most of them. "I could tell if something was wrong soon enough to stop," he says. "If something sounded funny or looked funny, I'd know." Then one of the older men would take over.

A tired moment during harvest.

Joel doesn't drive the corn picker at all, a machine that picks ear corn without shelling it. But he does help cut and rake cornstalks in a harvested field so they can be round-baled by the same machine that round-bales hay. The baled cornstalks will be used to bed livestock, keeping them dry and warm during the winter months ahead.

Wild animals, which have no human-packed bedding, are often seen during harvest as they prepare for winter. One day Joel saw a pheasant that had been scared from its hiding place by his approaching tractor. He also saw a coyote and then three deer, whose blond bodies—the color of cornstalks—bounded across the field and over a fence to the sanctuary of a wood.

Fortunately for the regional farmers, this harvest the price of corn was jumping as high as the deer. Severe summer drought in several states had hurt the corn crop and caused prices to rise. "The price of corn is up to $3.00 [per bushel] now," said Ed in August. "I've never had more than $2.60. If it gets to $3.20, I'll sell." In September it did, and Ed sold 8,000 bushels of corn to the Pillsbury Company.

Pillsbury is a busy merchant in autumn, buying millions of tons of corn grown in Midwestern fields and selling them throughout the world. One of its loading stations is on the Mississippi River in Dubuque, Iowa. From eight in the morning until midnight and sometimes later, trucks roll in, most hauling one thousand bushels of corn. The trucker Ed hired to haul his corn had to wait in line behind forty-four trucks before his turn came to dump the yellow cargo into a loading pit. From there it was transported up mechanical arms to a sliding floor, which carried it onto a waiting barge.

Ed's corn—which Joel had helped to cultivate in May and to harvest in October—now became part of a stream of grain that rained down on the barge at fifteen thousand bushels an hour until the pile

Ed sold some of his corn in September, before it was even picked.
Once the corn was harvested, this truck hauled it to the barges waiting
in Dubuque, Iowa, to take it overseas.

was fifteen feet deep. The full barge would float south to New Orleans. From there, its cargo would travel to the Gulf of Mexico and then overseas. Farmers in other countries would use it to fatten livestock, and industry would use it to make starch, paper, glue, sweetners, oil, or meal.

*The Hollands harvested five hundred acres of corn,
about seventy thousand bushels.*

Back home on Joel's farm, the rest of the corn crop fills crib, shed, and bin to the rafters. Once again the land tilled by James Holland over one hundred years ago has yielded corn in abundance. James could not have fathomed the measure. In his day, one farmer fed about ten people. Now he feeds sixty-one.

It takes seven wagonloads—half a day's work—to fill the crib.

The hard-working Holland team, and their machinery, in a harvested field.
From left: *Bill, Marty, Terry, Joel, Betty, Ed.*

Probably James could not have imagined the present costs of farming, either. A single tractor costs forty thousand dollars. A combine, used about thirty days a years, costs seventy thousand dollars. One acre of Holland land, for which James may have paid less than one hundred dollars, is now worth two thousand dollars.

Joel has the same easy-going attitude toward money that he has toward almost everything else. One day he was driving through the country with a friend when they passed by a farmer spreading manure in his cornfield.

"Smells bad," said the friend.

"Smells like money," said Joel jauntily.

No doubt, Joel will maintain his sense of humor even as he assumes the risks and the gambles of owning a farm. Though high prices prevent many young people from farming at all, Joel's place on the farm is nearly guaranteed. His father plans to retire from farming in eight years, when Joel graduates from college. Then, with his brothers Terry and Bill, Joel may rent or buy the ancestral farm.

If dreams are met, he will continue to farm with Bill and Terry, just as Ed does now. Together they will work all their shared land. Though he will have use of the family pool of machinery, he will still go heavily into debt. His brother Terry borrowed $150,000 when he began farming. He was nineteen years old then.

Joel's desire to keep farming is not for high profits, but for the way of life it offers. If he were able to have a desk job making fifty thousand dollars a year, no overtime—would he give up farming for that? "I'd probably take it for a couple years so I could save and buy my own farm," he answers.

Yet it is more than his determination and more than financial support that insure Joel's place on the farm if he wants it. Most important are his skills. When Joel begins farming on his own, he will harvest a lifetime of learning.